W9-BIZ-474
ccep
9/2011

The Summer Visitors

by Karel Hayes

This book is dedicated to my editor, Michael Steere, without whose persistent "nagging" I would never have done this book. Thank you, Michael, for this and all of your wonderful help over the past five years.

ISBN 978-0-89272-918-0

Printed in China

54321

Library of Congress Cataloging-in-Publication Information
available upon request

Distributed to the trade by National Book Network
Manufacturer's Information:
O.G. Printing Productions, Ltd.
Kowloon, Hong Kong
Manufactured in May 2011

In early summer,

the summer visitors

will return.

Hooray,

hooray,

for everyone!

All summer long,

they will have so much fun,

they'll little care

who else has come

to stay

and share

their cottage.

In the fall they'll say goodbye

and leave
the cottage
far behind.

Goodbye, goodbye,

until next summer.